The Amazing Tale of Gwennie

Homeless to Palace

BASTET PUBLISHING

Thomas H Murray

CONTENTS

DEDICATION

Gwennie asked me to dedicate her life adventure to all the humans who touched her life and helped her along her way.

CHAPTER ONE

Gwennie was born to the only litter of her mixed parents. Her mother, Euterpe (Terpsie to her friends), was a wild, strong-willed Maine Coon cat living in a scrubland state park in southern California. Her father, Nuno, was an adventurous, ever-romantic Iberian lynx who traveled to southern California with his best friend, Figo, on a tramp steamer from his native Portugal.

Nuno met Figo, a streetwise ship rat, on the voyage from Lisboa to Long Beach, passing through many ports in between. They agreed on a deal that Nuno would not eat Figo and, in exchange, Figo would be his guide to all the important things along the way. They eventually became best friends and settled down in southern California together.

One day, Figo felt his inevitable end approaching. He left his feline family for one last journey that he could only do alone. This part of the story was well-documented in a previous tale of peril and adventure (The Adventures of Nuno and Figo: A Strange Journey of Two Unlikely Friends).

Nuno could not grieve for long. He had a family to feed. Hunting furry scrubland and forest folk soon took his mind off his loss. He took his daughter with him on these hunting trips, the only child cat still living with her parents.

She loved her father and learned quickly how to hunt for herself. She knew which prey was worth the energy and which not. Others were dangerous and to be shunned at all costs. One such animal to avoid was the rattlesnake.

One hot day she wandered away from Nuno and came across a strange round flat animal. It coiled itself into a round pile of its own body, sunning itself. She came up close to have a sniff. Suddenly, it woke up, raised its head, and made an evil sounding rattle from its tail.

Kitten froze, not sure what to do. She knew no fear, except for coyotes. She carefully approached the snake, her curiosity taking over her common sense. It had such a curious smell, after all. Just as the snake was preparing to strike, Nuno rushed from the bushes nearby and growled loudly. The snake turned to see what this new threat was and struck at the quickly advancing Nuno.

Nuno leaped out of range of the striking snake, and before it could recoil, Nuno pounced. Biting its neck put a sudden end to the snake. Nuno was quite upset with his daughter, but also proud that she was not a fearful house cat. He explained that she should never approach anything that looked like the now dead snake. He told her to take a bite so that she would learn that they do not even taste good.

When they returned home, she would ride on Nuno's back like Figo used to do. Nuno transferred all his love for Figo to his daughter. They went everywhere and did everything together.

Terpsie was not jealous, but she knew that one day soon their daughter would also leave and that might break Nuno's heart a second time. But there was nothing she could do or say to him. As for Nuno, he just banished from his mind her explanations and warnings. He did not want to even think about it.

It was because of this that he refused to name her. He had the superstitious idea that if he named her, she would grow up and leave. But without a name she would stay the little kitten that she was clearly no longer to anyone else.

As for Terpsie, she did not mind too much. She had never met a male who stuck around like Nuno had. As long as their nameless daughter stayed, Nuno would, too. But if she left, then Nuno would probably do so soon after. Male cats, big or small, were never known to be monogamous.

Terpsie knew all too well that there were numerous jealous females lurking about, especially the bored rich ones who lived up in the houses on the hills around their scrubland home. She knew she had the best male cat in all of southern California. She was also receiving messages from her body that it would be soon time to start another family and would need Nuno's undivided attention.

Meanwhile, Nuno would continue hunting with the nameless kitten on his back, who was now getting heavier every day. Sometimes they would meet her siblings in the wild space. Nuno would walk up to them and touch noses. They would stifle a purr trying to look all tough and grown up to their dad. Their sister would jump down and wrestle with them for a while until they remembered they were no longer kittens and break it off with a strong clawless bat on her ears. Then they would part ways until the next time their paths would cross in the large but limited expanse of their domain.

At six months old, the kittens were already as large as normal grown cats. Yet, Nuno insisted on carrying his favorite kitten on his back. This slowed him down, but he did not mind. Carrying her this way reminded him of his dearly missed friend Figo, whom he knew he would never see again.

4

Alas, this idyllic life was not to continue. The vagaries of life intervened early one evening. Nuno wanted to continue hunting for rabbits near the office park at the eastern edge of his territory. Kitten said, "Come on, Dad, we have enough for today."

"No, just one more. Can't have too many. I remember still how in the old country we never had enough. Some days, we would have nothing to eat at all. Look, there's one. I'll catch him. Hold on!"

Nuno sprang after a particularly fat rabbit. He could not run so fast with Kitten on his back, but still was gaining on the rabbit. It ran across the road to the safety of the bushes on the other side. Nuno followed in hot pursuit. Just then, a car was passing by and before Nuno could react, hit him on his hindquarters. Kitten flew into the air and into the bushes on the side of the road. Nuno was knocked over to the other side.

Nuno struggled away with his hind hip broken, not understanding what even happened. Kitten was panting heavily in the bush, unhurt but stunned and dazed. The car stopped by the side of the road and the passenger got out.

Her husband, sitting in the driver's seat, yelled at her, "What are you doing, Fran? We hit something. So what?"

"Frank, what is wrong with you?"

"It looked like a coyote. It'll bite you."

"I must see what we just did. Ah, it's a cat. Its stunned. We have to take it to a vet and make sure nothing is wrong with it."

"Oh, come on! Leave it alone."

"Are you crazy? This is someone's cherished pet. We have to return it to its owner. What if someone hit our Fluffie? Wouldn't you want someone to try to find us? Throw me the blanket in the back."

"Oh, for crying out loud, Fran! OK, here."

Fran wrapped Kitten up in the blanket and sat in the back seat. "Take us to our vet's animal hospital."

Kitten was still too dazed to know what happened. But as they approached the vet's office, she started to sense something was very wrong. She tried to struggle, but Fran held her tightly in the well wrapped blanket. Strange smells and sounds surrounded her. She started to wail, something she had never done before.

They rushed into the emergency room while Frank waited in the car. Fran explained to the vet what had happened. The vet unwrapped the blanket holding Kitten down on the examination table. This was too much. Kitten redoubled her most baleful cries that broke Fran's heart to hear. For the first time in her life, Nuno was nowhere near to explain patiently what was happening.

The vet had on his bite-proof gloves and felt all around Kitten's body. He took X-rays of her and concluded that she was, in fact, fine.

"Oh, God, what a relief. What can you tell me about her?" Fran asked. "Can we tell who the owner is? Does she have a chip?"

"She has no chip. She appears to be a six- or seven-months old Maine Coon cat. It appears she is feral. If you care about her, you could take her home and observe her for a week or so to make sure she is fine. Then you can either release her back into the wild or keep her. Whatever you decide, I suggest bringing her back here before you decide and have her operation to neuter her. We should also give her vaccinations. She has worms and fleas. I will give her two shots to take care of those. Meanwhile, do not let her out of the house."

"Fleas and worms? Glad Frank's not here to hear that."

"Don't worry. The shots took care of both problems. Here is a flea comb. You can comb the dead fleas and their eggs out of her

6

fur. You can feed her normal wet cat food. Of course, make sure she has sufficient water."

"Right. I'll take her home. Hope Fluffie doesn't mind cats."

"She is as big as he is now. In a few more months, she will grow to be twice as big as him."

"She is the first cat I ever had. How will I house train her?"

"You don't need to with cats. Just show her the cat box with litter and she'll understand what to do with it. I'll give you a cat carrier, so you don't have to hold her in the blanket for the ride home. It's a miracle that you hit her without hurting her seriously."

"You know that's the strange thing. It happened so fast. She was with another cat, but it was twice as big as her, almost the size of a coyote. We definitely hit it hard and what's completely crazy? I thought we cut it in two as one half went to one side of the road and the other half to the other. I could not find the other half, though there were signs of blood. We might have hit two animals that were connected somehow."

"Well, the blood didn't come from our lucky one here. You can pick up a cat box, litter, and everything else you will need right here. Sam at the counter will fix you up. Tell him to give you plenty of treats, too. Make an appointment for her operation and vaccinations in about a week. If you have any problems, give us a call. And remember, you will need a lot of patience, kindness, and treats to adopt a feral cat, if that's what you decide in the end. Hopefully, she's still young enough to learn that people can actually be good."

"Thanks for everything, Doctor."

She picked up all what the vet suggested and made an appointment for a week later. Back in the car, she explained everything to her husband, except the part about fleas and worms.

"All right, but we'll keep her for only a week. You know I never liked cats."

"For a week. Who knows? You might grow to like her."

"Doubt it." And they returned home, about five miles from the scene of the accident.

Fran set up the cat box and showed Kitten. Just then, Fluffie came running up, tail wagging, nose sniffing, all curious about the new animal. With a growl and a bat across the nose, Fluffie understood at once that it would take longer to win her over.

"Did you see what she did to Fluffie? I don't like her already." Frank sniffed.

"They must learn each other. It'll take time."

Kitten, for her part, ran and hid under the nearest bed. She stayed there for the rest of the day and into the next. She wailed herself to sleep. The whole experience was just too much. She went to sleep hoping that when she awoke, she would be back with her beloved parents in their family den. When hunger woke her in the middle of the night, she was tempted to escape and return to the forest to find something to eat. But she still did not dare leave the safety of under the bed.

The next day, Fran tried to coax her out with a plate of cat food. Kitten was having nothing to do with. It smelled interesting, but it did not appear nor smell like any animal she had ever seen. A hiss and a growl sent Fran away. But she placed the food with water in the far corner of the room, so Kitten would have to leave the safety of beneath the bed to get to it.

The next night, her hunger forced her out from under the bed and, being sure no one was nearby, she suspiciously approached the food and water. She sniffed and sniffed but could discover nothing wrong with either. She ate and drank her full. Back under the bed, she felt a powerful urge to relieve herself. She remembered the cat box. There was nothing else around close to what she had previously used to cover her tracks. She crept out and found it.

Kitten properly buried her treasures and was on her way back to the safety of the bed when she met Fluffie. She again hissed and growled, warning him off. Fluffie tried a different approach. He whined in a most pathetic way. Kitten thought she might have hurt him and gave him a sniff at his nose. Fluffie sniffed back and thought he found a new friend. So, what does a dog do with a new friend? He sniffed her backside. That produced another growl with a hard bat across the nose. Fluffie ran away, whimpering.

Kitten decided Fluffie could become a satisfying meal one day and therefore might have a use after all. Back under the bed, she slept until Fran woke her up the next morning, offering her treats. Now this was something special that caught Kitten's attention. There was no way she would eat anything from Fran's hand. So, Fran left them on the floor one by one, creating a trail of delight away from the bed to the living room.

Now the idea of eating something that was not alive immediately before was totally strange to Kitten, yet she could eat them without the hassle of hunting. She decided that this could be a good thing. She followed the fragrant trail. Fluffie whined behind the closed door of another bedroom. Frank was away at work. It was just Fran trying her hardest to bond with the very strange cat that suddenly entered their lives.

It took the rest of the day for Kitten to allow her to approach, but still not close enough to pet. Many dozens of treats later, Kitten jumped up on the sofa and laid down. Fran sat on the other end and talked to her in the nicest way, like to a baby. Three days into this strange experience, she decided that the strange woman was harmless and so was the idiot dog. She had not made up her mind about Frank, who seemed angry all the time.

Frank proved this when he came home from work. He entered the front door and saw them sitting on the sofa. "Get that cat off the sofa! Not even Fluffie can sit on the sofa or the bed. What are you thinking, Fran?"

Kitten jumped off the sofa and ran back under the bed. Fran yelled at him, "Now do you see what you did? I have been trying all day to gain her trust and now you've ruined it!"

"Why? In a few more days, we'll be rid of her."

"What's wrong with you? Have you no heart?" And she stopped talking to Frank the rest of the day. That just irritated Frank even more.

Fran continued her efforts the next day. After five days of being in the strange new house, Kitten allowed Fran to pet her. Fran knew enough about cats to know they love being stroked under their chin and cheeks. Kitten felt like she always had an itch there. Before she knew it, she let herself go and started to purr. Between treats and chin scratches, she decided she liked Fran.

With the sound of purring, Fran knew she had finally succeeded in winning over the strange wild cat's trust. "Now, you beautiful animal, I must give you a name. I think I will name you 'Guinevere'. You won the hearts of King Arthur's knights." With that, she decided she would keep Guinevere, or Guinnie, for short.

CHAPTER TWO

The day of the operation arrived, and Guinevere allowed herself to be put back in her cat carrier, but then immediately regretted it. She cried all the way to the animal hospital. The operation went smoothly, and she left fully vaccinated. The vet asked Fran if she wanted a microchip inserted to prove ownership. She almost said yes, but then she remembered she was not sure if she could win the fight with her husband about keeping her. Frank's complete dislike of Guinevere seriously vexed her. She had agreed that she would keep the cat until her operation.

"What now? Can I put her back into the wild?" Fran asked.

"Oh, no. You better wait until she has fully recovered from her operation. Come back in ten days and I'll remove the stitches."

"Oh, thank you! I mean, um… thanks for everything." She was glad to know that doctor's orders prevented her from letting Guinevere go just yet. But she also knew that with every passing day together, it would be more difficult to part ways.

Frank could not hide his anger when she told him they had to keep her another ten days. When she stopped talking to him, he knew he could not win this one, being based on medical advice that did make sense. Guinevere was sitting in the center of the living room, trying to come to her senses while the anesthesia wore off.

Frank was still wearing his leather shoes for work. He walked to his favorite comfy chair to watch TV. Guinevere was in his path, and he flicked her out of the way with his foot. This caused her such pain that she released one of her baleful cries. From then on, Guinevere would always have a fear of a man wearing leather dress shoes. Fran came out of the kitchen and guessed what had happened.

"You hurt that cat one more time and you'll be sleeping on the sofa for many months." Fran seethed at him.

About thirty minutes later, returning from the bathroom, he did the same again to her. Fran picked up a vase and threw it right at his head. He ducked, and it smashed against the wall behind him.

"I'm serious, you bastard! On the sofa for you. Now, clean it up!" Fran was furious.

She then picked her Guinnie up carefully in her arms, carried her into their bedroom, and locked the door. She could not believe that she had formed such an attachment to the cat that was now stronger than to her husband. But why does he have to be such a petty bastard, hurting an innocent animal? She started to see him in a new light.

As for Frank, it was not really about the cat, though he hated the damn thing well enough. It was more about his wife disobeying him. She never defied him before like this, and she certainly never became violent over anything. Fine, he told himself. He would wait another week for the cat to heal and then he would demand her expulsion. Meanwhile, he had to sleep the best he could on the sofa.

Ten days passed, and Guinevere healed. The vet removed her stitches and proclaimed her a healthy cat with no ailments, worms, or fleas. She had been sleeping on the bed with Fran, absent Frank. Without even trying, she had won Fran's heart.

There was another big fight that evening with Frank when she told him she decided to keep Guinnie. Frank went ballistic. Fran was silent, staring at him with enraged eyes. After a full minute, she spoke in a very quiet but firm voice, "Frank, are you willing to destroy our marriage over a cat? Because that's exactly what you are doing."

This stopped Frank in his furious tracks. He realized he had gone too far. No, he was not willing to end his marriage over a cat. A disrespectful wife was another matter. He went outside for a walk and decided that he would have to seek his revenge indirectly. In the meantime, he would bide his time with the damn cat.

He was all apologetic when he returned and prepared the sofa for sleeping. The next days he tried to be nice to Guinnie, even tried to give her some beloved treats, but she refused anything from his hand. But Fran noticed and decided to give him another week on the sofa before letting him back to bed.

Months went by and Frank's plan had finally fallen into place. He accepted a promotion that required him to move to Santa Barbara. They found a delightful house overlooking the ocean from the hills and put their Lake Forest home up for sale. Fran was excited about the move and happy with Frank again, who seemed to have completely changed his attitude to Guinnie.

Moving day arrived, and boxes were piled everywhere. The moving men and van would arrive in a few hours and there was still much to pack. Frank noticed they needed more packing materials, or they would never get it all done in time. He sent Fran off with a shopping list.

As soon as she left, Frank brought out from hiding a new cat carrier and stuffed Guinnie inside. He drove about five miles east to where the suburbia of Orange County met the dry hill lands, and he dropped her off by the bicycle path, still locked inside the cat carrier. He figured someone would find her and take her home with them. After all, he did not consider himself cruel.

Six hours later, after everything was packed into the moving van, they loaded the car. It was then that Fran realized Guinnie was missing. She frantically searched the empty house everywhere. Frank played along. He looked everywhere with her.

"She must have ran out of the house during all the moving. The moving men must have scared her."

They searched outside all through the neighborhood. Calling her name until it got dark.

"Come on, honey, we have to get going. I'm sorry about Guinnie as much as you are."

Fran sat on the front steps and sobbed uncontrollably. A neighbor came over and asked what was wrong. Frank replied with much feigned sorrow that their cat went missing in the hustle bustle of the move. Had he seen their cat anywhere? No, he had not, but he would call them if he did.

Frank tried to console his wife, even offering to get another cat for her in their new home. In the end, the cat never really mattered. He won the struggle with his wife in the end, and that was enough. Fran knew that no other cat could ever replace her beloved Guinnie. Gradually, she controlled her grief and fell for her husband's reasonable logic. She let him take her to the car and drive away.

As for Guinnie, a jogger passed by and stopped when he heard her cries. He opened the door to the cat carrier, allowing her to leap away into the bushes. She had heard the faint cries of her mistress carried by the evening wind. Judging the direction, she ran towards it and away from the strange wilderness she had suddenly found herself. Guinnie could have easily made the scrubland her new home, but it never occurred to her. She had to find Fran!

There were too many busy roads and rows of houses to cross. Her mistress's cries eventually stopped and by the time Guinnie found her way back home, it was dark and empty. There was no way to enter, and no one heeded her cries to open the door.

The neighbor noticed her the next day and put out food for her. He called Frank and told him that their cat had returned. Frank replied with thanks and asked him to feed it, but that they do not really want her back.

"But your wife seemed so sad about it," the neighbor replied.

"Yes, but she has a new cat now and the stress of the move was too much for her. She should have increased the dose of her medication." Etc. Etc. That was the end of it.

The neighbor did indeed put food out when he remembered, but his wife was allergic to cats and so could never let her live with them. Once again, Guinnie found herself living in the wild. But this wild was a small woods surrounded by a loose circle of houses.

The houses had crawl spaces for storage underneath, most without any kind of door. This is where she found her shelter. She had to rely on the kindness of strangers for food and when that was in short supply, rabbits, birds, and squirrels would suffice, just as in her early days. But she always kept the house in view, waiting for her mistress to return.

Sunning herself on the uncut lawn of the front yard, Guinnie considered her situation; weighed her options. She thought perhaps it would be better to call off the failed experiment with people and find her way back to the protected scrubland of her birth. She could rejoin her parents and help hunt rabbits. Her father surely had recovered from the accident. Her heart raced at the warm memories. She leaped up, ready to hurry back. But where to go?

She had no idea in which direction was her loving den. It was a long trek from where she was abandoned just to return to her human home. She had to contend with the busy streets of fast-moving cars. Then there were the endless houses with their fences holding back aggressive dogs, requiring her to make countless detours. The long journey became much longer. Her heart shrank at the very thought.

In the end, she decided it was worth a try. She discovered that past two rows of houses divided by a quiet dead-end street and up an embankment was a pair of long iron rails that disappeared into the distance to her left and right. They appeared to cut through all the suburban clutter. But which direction was her homeland? The fiercely foul smell of the rails eliminated any possibility of following her nose.

As she pondered this mystery, an Amtrak train quickly approached where she was standing, sending her fleeing for cover of the trees. What was that evil thing? Clearly, the iron rails would offer no hope. Back to her warm sunny grass patch, she slowly came to realize that she only had one choice. She had to wait for her mistress to return. Surely, she would soon.

Fortunately, the law forbade dogs from running loose. They were confined to fenced in backyards. They were very loud barking versions of the quiet coyote that killed several of her fellow kittens when she was still innocent of any threats to an idyllic life in the little den, she called her first home.

Occasionally, a real coyote would appear, clearly lost, and confused at a very wrong turn it made from the dry hills to the east. If it saw her, the perplexed look in its eyes was a call for help, not at all threatening. If Guinnie had fingers, she would have gladly pointed it in the right direction and far away from her peaceful, wooded space.

There were others who were not at all lost but fortunately were content to leave her alone. These were raccoons and opossums. They were about the same size as Guinnie. Their only crime was to eat the food left for her by the neighboring houses. She had to be on the alert for when the random food would appear. Luckily for her, the humans were daytime animals, and her competitors were mainly active at night.

The raccoons and opossums were not above eating from carelessly covered trash cans. Hunger would sometimes force her to do the same. She could sniff through the remains and usually found something not too offensive. Her father ridiculed the practice, though he never told her he did the very same on his journey from Portugal.

Guinnie settled into a routine. She made the rounds of the houses that had left food for her. If it had been a while since they put food out, she would sun herself on their back decks, reminding them of their duty. This often worked, to her amazement. She was learning the ancient feline art of human manipulation.

Then one day the peaceful quiet of deep suburbia (only regularly broken by obnoxious leaf blowers) was destroyed by a large moving truck backing up to the front of the house. A small group of men carried furniture and boxes into her newly opened home. Had her mistress returned after what seemed an eternity ago? The garage door was open, but Guinnie certainly did not dare to enter with so many strange people moving about. She hid in the bushes, waiting for her mistress to appear. But she never did.

CHAPTER THREE

Though it seemed like years, about a month later, a younger couple moved in. Jack was in his late thirties and Svetlana in her late twenties. Once again, the house was filled with life. Guinnie could sense that the woman did not like cats. In truth, Svetlana was frightened of them ("they might bite"), despite growing up in a small apartment in southern Ukraine with a huge Rottweiler dominating the small space, who actually did bite her, sending her to the hospital. As for a pet, they could only agree to a small tortoise.

Jack loved cats, but Guinnie already had one experience when one half of a couple liked them while the other did not. Guinnie could not trust anyone who obviously had no sense in choosing such a mate. The fact he had no sense was unclear to Jack at the time, but for different reasons he would later discover. When Guinnie would sometimes sun herself on the front lawn, she would run away whenever Jack tried to approach her. He clearly did not understand the attraction of delicious treats. But he would, in good time.

Guinnie was a beautiful cat. Though she did not understand that, Jack did. With beautiful parents of an Iberian Lynx father and a Maine Coon cat mother, Guinnie was twice as big as normal house cats. Not just in size, she weighed eighteen and a half pounds (eight kilograms). Her long fur had the colors of her father and tortoise shell/calico mother. Her soft underbelly was a light blonde, becoming darker to a black that covered the top of her body. She had the typical fluff growing from between the pads of her feet like a hobbit. She carried her furry duster tail high: the proud banner of long-haired cats everywhere. Her beautiful green eyes were framed in a great ruff that would have made her lynx father proud.

After almost ten years, another woman moved in, replacing the younger one. She had more of a heart for the poor homeless animals in the area. Her name was Janet, and she started putting food and water outside the front door. But now Guinnie had to share this food with two younger feral male cats. Because of her operation, Guinnie had no interest in male cats, generally holding them in disdain like she did with all male hominids. For their part, they simply ignored her hissings while pushing her aside from the generous food offerings.

White Socks was a black cat with, well, white paws. He was older and warier of the humans than his opponent. Little Blue was a younger Russian Blue who was more adventurous. Once he entered the open kitchen door. Jack and Janet watched, hoping he would make their home his. But when he backed up to the dining table leg with tail held high and twitching, preparing to mark the kitchen as his territory, they shooed him out the door. During this time, Jack and Janet unknowingly called Guinnie 'Fluffy', like Fran's pet dog. They were not very imaginative with names. Of course, none of the cats were part of the family yet.

Though ignoring her, the two boys viciously fought each other all the time over the food that was neither theirs nor scarce. Since they never knew the comfort of having a warm home like Guinnie did, they had no intention of ever reciprocating the kindness of their free food. But Guinnie continued, nay, yearned for the comfort of being part of a family, of having a home. She hoped with a more sympathetic woman that maybe, just maybe, this couple might be the answer. Yet, how could she trust them? Regular food is a start, but she needed more proof.

One night in January, she decided to test them. She jumped onto the roof in the front part of the house, where it is only six feet (about two meters) above the ground. She could easily and often did jump the twelve feet (about four meters) height of the back deck, but this idea was the best she could come up with.

Despite there being a large pepper tree right next to the roof, which she could effortlessly climb down. She cried out into the cold darkness, "I'm stuck. I can't get down. In the name of all the goddesses, will someone please help me!"

All Jack and Janet heard were the signature baleful cries of 'Fluffy'. They came out to see what the commotion was all about. There, perched on the roof's edge, was a damsel in distress, crying to be saved. This was the correct manipulative test.

Jack disappeared to get the ladder from the garage. During the brief time Jack had disappeared, Guinnie thought they failed her simple test. She disappeared into the darkness, disappointed. But then the ladder arrived, and Janet climbed up. Guinnie reappeared into the light and allowed Janet to carry her down the ladder. But once Janet placed her on the ground, she instantly disappeared into the night.

The rescuers looked at each other in surprise. What was that all about? They both had seen how Guinnie effortlessly sprang up and down from the much higher deck. Before leaping up, she would tilt back slightly on the powerful springs of her hind legs and jump the exact distance to the deck. Landing on her feet from a jump down only resulted in a slight lowering of her body like shock absorbers on a car.

What it was all about became clear the next night. It was raining, cold for southern California. When Janet opened the front door to place the usual dishes of food and water, Guinnie followed her heart and sprinted into the house. Jack and Janet were taken entirely by surprise and not prepared with even a cat box. So, Guinnie had to spend the first night in the cold garage. She found a protected place to sleep on the pile of neatly stacked firewood, off the cold concrete floor. There were food and water dishes, but no cat box. She could hold it until the next day; otherwise, behind the wood pile she would go.

In the dark but dry garage, Guinnie considered what she had just done and what would come of it. She was optimistic about the couple. Janet clearly cared for her by making sure she had food and water. But the real question was Jack. Over the years, she had been studying Jack from the distance and had a good feeling about him. She decided to rely on her feline intuition, which can tell who a cat lover is and who is not. She congratulated herself on the success of her manipulation, realizing how easy it was to bend humans to her cat will. No matter what, she could always flee back into the relative safety of her little woods. It was worth a try.

Guinnie was learning the universal logic of domestic cats: anything desired is worth trying for. The worse that can happen is they would say 'no' with maybe a clapping of hands or a stomping of a foot. Looking adorable would always help in this quest.

Early the next day, Jack and Janet made a quick trip to the local pet store. Once they were prepared with all things a cat would need, Guinnie was once again allowed to roam her home freely. The furniture was different and in different places, but she recognized everything else: the wood-burning fireplace, the wooden floors, the Mexican tiles of the hallways, the exceptionally large deck wrapping around the back of the house. The warm sun patches on the carpet were in the same places.

At first, she thought it was a trap when they tried to get her to sit on the sofa or on the bed. Frank always threw things at her or otherwise roughly threw her off sofas and beds. Gwennie would always turn to him with a hiss and growl, "If you don't want me to sleep on sofas and beds, why did you put them in my home to begin with?"

Interestingly, it was Jack who understood cats better than Janet. Jack's best friend growing up was a semi-wild calico, who would follow him through the Pennsylvania forests like a dog with its master. Jack was no more than a kitten himself when his mother brought home a kitten that someone had left in a box with her siblings at a petrol station. The two near babies grew up together. As for Janet, she grew up on a farm in fox-hunting hound-loving Ireland where cats would very often end up in sacks tossed into the rivers.

So, Jack made sure that one of the things they picked up at the pet store were cat treats. As luck would have it, they were the same treats Fran had found. Jack knew that the great feline manipulators could be manipulated themselves. The crinkling sound of Guinnie's favorite treat bag opening always perked her ears up. The familiar smell (like freshly cooked popcorn with melted butter to humans) enticed her to gradually overcome her fear. She would literally do anything for treats.

The fly in the ointment was confusing. Jack cared for and understood her much better than Janet did. But the fact was, Jack was still a man. Her only experience with a man was unfortunately too traumatic at too early an age to get over. As with Frank, whenever Jack wore his leather shoes, she ran for cover under the bed.

Her memory of being kicked by similar shoes always created panic in her heart. This was rare, as Jack would put on his street shoes just before leaving the house and only wore slippers or went barefoot in the house, depending on the time of year. But sometimes he would forget something after stepping outside and he would quickly reenter with his shoes still on to retrieve it. This would inevitably send Guinnie scrambling for cover.

Even so, her new life back in her old home with different humans was turning out to be fine. She settled into their typical strange routines. They fed her like they ate themselves, three times a day. They disappeared into slumber the whole night through. Not even baleful cries at three in the morning could make them get up to give her treats. She already understood what a cat box was for, and the universal domestic cat deal held. Humans promised to give cats a clean cat box, and cats, in turn, promised to use it. There was no need to walk a cat in an early cold, raining morning.

After a few months of settling in, Guinnie had her own routine. Eat and drink her fill in the morning. Use her cat box and then go roaming for the rest of the morning, searching for food left out by her other neighboring admirers. Jack always wondered why she did not do her business outside while roaming. Clearly Jack never used a cat box, and there is an enormous difference between standing behind any convenient tree or wall like a man and squatting behind bushes like a woman or a womanly cat. She would return for a quick nap and lunch before disappearing for the rest of the day.

Gradually, her lunchtime naps became longer. Guinnie increasingly felt lethargic. She had to think twice before vaulting up to the elevated deck. Jack correctly suspected the cause. He lifted her tail and saw dozens of what looked like cooked white rice kernels. Worms! They took her on a quick trip by car to see a veterinarian in a much-hated cat carrier. Guinnie cried all the way, remembering the last time she was in a similar situation, she was abandoned by the roadside.

Instead of being abandoned, she was given medicine to kill the worms and fleas that had made their home in her body again, sucking the vitality from her. A few weeks later, she once again had the energy she had known in her younger years. She was five years old, already in the prime of feline life. Though Jack and Janet might not have thought so, Guinnie understood perfectly the significance of what they did for her. She reveled in their love as she sat purring loudly on the sofa in front of a fire in the fireplace. She did not even mind Janet combing her fur with a tight flea comb, removing the vermin eggs. Janet was always gentle and followed up with very generous offerings of treats.

Despite their warm care, Guinnie still preferred to roam about her little kingdom, eating food from whomever put it out for her. Except for the warm shelter at night with her kind humans and an after-lunch siesta, she preferred to spend most of her time alone and away from them. Her independence was vitally important to her. She still did not want to become too attached to her humans. They were a nice convenience; not to be a necessity. They may disappear and leave her alone like the first ones did. Sure enough, within six months of Guinnie choosing them as her life mates, they did disappear.

CHAPTER FOUR

Jack had a short four-month consulting project in São Paulo, Brazil. Janet wanted to go with him. They could not take Guinnie with them, and they did not want to put her in a kennel until they returned. So, she found herself again living on her own. They did think enough to put several large containers of dry food on the dining table under the gazebo on the deck. But that lasted about three days until the raccoons discovered it. Once again, Guinnie had to rely on her wits and the kindness of strangers.

Guinnie's emotions ran the full range. First, she was confused. The house was dark, and the doors shut. What could that mean? Where were they? Then confusion turned to anger. What is it with humans? They win her trust and then abandon her, tossing her back into the woods to survive on her own.

Eventually, her anger turned to worry, even panic. Would they never come back? Many kind neighbors stopped putting food out for her when they saw she had found a home to live. Sometimes with great shame she would eat the leftovers from a trashcan the racoons had knocked over and picked through. Again, she considered searching for her childhood scrubland. It had already been many years, and she doubted she could find her way there, even more so since when she first considered it.

About a month later, she resigned herself to the hard life of a cat living on her own: hungry, surrounded by plenty. She got by with an occasional bird or squirrel. Since every house's lawn had a sprinkler system, water was never a problem. The neighbor's house across the open wooded space still did not have a door blocking the entrance to the crawl space under the house. Guinnie returned to the same dry place out of the elements to sleep where she had lived before. Though far from perfect, she at least could get by. In time, she only occasionally wondered if they would ever return.

Yet they did return. The first thing Jack did when he walked in the door was to grab the treat bag and head out to the back deck. He called for Guinnie. She popped out from under her space under the neighbor's house, ran a few steps and then stopped. Could it be? Did they return? She could not trust her eyes. Then Jack wrinkled the treaty bag, signaling that her favorite thing in the world was again available. The sound triggered something in her heart. She came bounding back through the trees, leaping up on to the high deck with the grace that only cats have.

Her people were back and happy to see her. Everything was right with the world again. She decided she would no longer accept food from anyone else but them. Jack noticed this and decided to change her name. Guinnie told him in the beginning that her human-given name was Guinevere. But he changed it to Gwendolyn. Guinevere, he explained to his beloved cat, was a fickle, treacherous woman, the wife of King Arthur and lover of Lancelot, his right-hand man. She caused her husband's death and the downfall of the kingdom. But not to worry. Gwendolyn was also a Welsh name with the diminutive 'Gwennie' sounding practically the same as 'Guinnie'.

He also explained that his cat-fearing ex-wife was too close to being a Guinevere herself, too close for comfort. The two stories had too much in common, except the part about the king dying. Gwennie would be her new name. Gwennie did not understand all the history or even what an 'ex' was. She answered to it just the same. She had two other names. One was 'Kitten' that her dear old dad called her, and the other is still a secret.

Jack continued doing his consulting projects with clients around north America, returning home on weekends. Janet stayed home, living a life of leisure with Gwennie. Often joining Gwennie sunbathing nude on the back deck. California wine and herb kept her warm. Life was good for both of them.

There were several reasons why Gwennie became closer to Janet than to Jack. Janet would give her treats by the handful, not counting them out like Jack did. Jack was only around on weekends. Most important of all was he still suffered from the handicap of being a man. Gwennie slept next to Janet in the sun on the deck, on the sofa, and on the bed at night. She followed Janet around like a little satellite.

One weekend afternoon, Jack was surveying the woods from the deck. A neighbor was walking his dog. The dog noticed White Paws and went berserk. Incredibly, the man released the dog, egging it on with the words: "Go sic 'em, boy!"

White Paws had an injured front paw at the time and tried to escape, limping as fast as he could. Jack could see the panic in his eyes. Jack yelled to the dog-owner, "What the hell are you doing? Get that dog back on a leash! I'm calling Animal Control. How would you like it if someone attacked your pet?"

"Oh, sorry. I thought it was a stray or feral or something." As if that would have made it any better. He called for his dog to return, which, of course, it would not. White Paws climbed up the side of a tree and clung on to the bark for dear life. The man, both angry and embarrassed, approached his dog, leashed it, and pulled it away. An hour later, White Paws tentatively came down from the tree and disappeared. Jack and Janet never saw him again.

CHAPTER FIVE

Six months later, Gwennie's life became seriously strange. She and her humans moved to Jiangyin, an industrial city in China on the Yangtze River (Chang Jiang) about two hours northwest of Shanghai. She had to spend the first two weeks in jail (quarantine) before they released her. The flight, the jail time, her new home in an apartment were all just too much. She became an indoor cat after all that. Her humans tried to take her for walks in the park, putting her on a leash. She always managed to squirm out of the leash and then hide under a bush. Thankfully, her humans gave up on that idea.

They moved to a new apartment a year after they arrived in China. Gwennie told Jack she did not like the idea. "Why do we have to move? I still don't understand why we're in China in the first place."

"I explained many times to you, my sweet. I am the President of this company, and this is where our factory is. It's an interesting job and a great professional challenge. As for why we have to move, you need to ask the landlord. The new apartment has more light and is closer to the factory, anyway."

"You know, none of that makes any sense to me, nor does Marx's theory of forces and relations of production. No need for lectures. I thought we were doing fine in southern California."

"Forces of production? The ridiculous things you say sometimes, silly kitty. I'm no Marxist. It simply is a good career move. The simplest explanation is that you love treaties, and treaties cost money. Since I don't see you making any money, nor is Janet, for that matter, it's up to me to keep it all together."

"I'm just saying that we had no shortage of treaties before China. Besides, what kind of work could I do, other than just being adorable? Would anyone pay for that?"

"Look, we've discussed this before. I could rent you out as a pillow. You would be perfect. You're just the right size and you're soft and warm. If you purred, we could charge extra. That would be the perfect white noise to fall asleep to. Every time I try to use you as my pillow, you get restless and struggle to escape after just a few minutes."

"I refuse to be a pillow, yours or any stranger's. OK, whatever. Here we are. Just will have to make the most of it. Just promise me we'll not be here forever. I don't even trust this new place."

Jack held her in his arms and introduced her to each new room, proving that there were no bugaboos anywhere.

When the tour was complete, Gwennie spoke into Jack's ear, "OK, OK, I get it. Now put me down so I can sniff around myself."

They had a stick with a feather tied on a long string at the end. Gwennie loved to chase and pounce on it. Jack would swirl the feather in a circle behind her, and Gwennie would do back-flips pursuing it through the air. Otherwise, she would nap on her back with her four furry paws extended and curled. She sprawled and lounged on the bed, sofa, certain comfy chairs, etc.

Eventually, they had to wash the covers used to catch her long, luxurious fur that she would leave everywhere. One day, the washing machine's drain became clogged, and Jack had to call the landlord. He arrived with a plumber. The plumber found the problem in no time and cleared it up. After he explained it to the landlord, the landlord turned to Jack and told him he should stop washing the cat in the washing machine.

Jack thought that was possibly one of the funniest things he ever heard. Stifling a laugh, he solemnly vowed that he would never do such a thing again. The only solution was they just had to remove as much fur as they could by hand before washing the covers.

After the plumber and landlord left, Jack translated their conversation. Janet agreed that was indeed hilarious. Gwennie was horrified and ran under the bed. Jack was bilingual in Mandarin as he was an Asian studies major at the University of Chicago and had attended Furen University in Taiwan in his early twenties. This was yet another reason why he was a perfect fit to run the China operations of a US company.

Dealing with the stressful challenge of turning around a failing factory was what made the work interesting. Even dealing with the typical cliquish divisions in a Chinese factory and other culture-based challenges was not insurmountable. The success shown on the bottom line made Jack feel good about himself. It was professional satisfaction.

The anger-inducing stress came from dealing with the unprofessional idiots in the home office in Phoenix, Arizona. One night, on one of Jack's weekly Skype calls with his father in the US, recounting a particularly offensive interaction with the CEO, Jack's anger flared, and he pounded the desk.

He was sitting in an armchair in his home office with his computer. Gwennie ran to him. She stood on her back paws with one front paw, supporting herself on the arm of the chair. With her other front paw, she patted Jack's forearm and gave him a plaintive meow. "Oh, deary pip, please calm down. It's not so bad, is it?"

Jack had no choice but to get a hold of himself. Even so, he knew he had to start thinking of a future away from that company. Despite having made a failing company successful and putting tens of millions into the pocket of the owner, they were not paying him enough for the aggravation. Besides, after paying both US and Chinese income taxes, he really was not getting ahead.

Besides all that, Gwennie caught some kind of skin disease that baffled every veterinarian. Eventually, they had to shave all the magnificent fur off her back for the medicine to be effective. That was the last straw. They decided to return to southern California, but not to the wonderful house Gwennie knew. Renters were living there then. They would live in an apartment in Murrieta, northeast of San Diego, close to the wine district of Temecula.

Going through Customs at LAX in her cat carrier in the luggage cart with her back still bare of fur, Jack told her to be silent and covered her carrier with a coat. She did not make a sound, even when a drug-searching beagle approached the coat and gave it a good sniff. Jack was worried that if the Customs people saw her shaved back, they may become suspicious and put her in quarantine. Thanks to her not making a peep, they walked right through and out into the California air.

"You were great, sweet kit."

"Thanks. You know how I hate beagles. I so wanted to open this thing and give his sniffing nose a good paw full of claws. It was all I could do to control myself."

"You would be assaulting a federal employee. That's a felony, and you would be doing time, hard time, not just quarantine."

"Yeah, well, that's kind of what kept me under control."

Gwennie saw little of Jack during their year in Murrieta. He was away, including many weekends, doing his consulting in places like Canada, the middle of Iowa in the winter, North Carolina, etc. Gwennie spent her days in peace and calm with Janet. Sitting with her on the sofa while she read her crime and spy novels. Sleeping under the covers with her at night. Laying in the sun on the balcony watching the birds at the bird feeder.

It was then that Jack discovered there are not just a northern California and a southern California, which differ greatly from each other. But, in fact, there is also an eastern California. That would be the area east of the ridge of mountains running north to south of the state. This area has more of a ranching culture of horses and guns. Much of the populace were refugees from the craziness that the western half was full of. They are closer to the ranching culture of Nevada and Arizona.

After a year there, they missed the western craziness and moved to another apartment in Ocean Beach, San Diego. Their apartment was directly above a beautiful young cannabis-smoking Brazilian couple with a baby. Jack knew this because smoke rises as it did directly to his home office above them. Fortunately, the baby was too stoned to wail. She was a biology researcher at the Salk Institute, and he surfed all day. Coming from a family who lived in the Le Jardin area of São Paulo, he did not have to concern himself with the uncool hassle of making money.

As before, the closest Gwennie ever came to being outdoors was to watch the birds at the birdfeeder on the balcony. She was even closer to Janet. Besides, Jack was by then always away doing consulting projects in foreign lands. Jack would work three weeks overseas with a week off back home. But in truth, it was Jack who loved her the most. Janet cared for Gwennie but would have preferred her to be a proper bird-retrieving dog.

Things would get worse before getting better. Janet decided she preferred to be with Jack wherever in the world he would be working. The three of them went to Cologne (Köln), Germany for another project. They all three lived in the many-starred Hilton Hotel in the center of the city. It was a small hotel room with a large bed where Gwennie would spend most of her time. She was slowing down now, being about sixteen years old. By the time they moved to a motel room at a truck stop near Ashtabula, Ohio for another project some months later, she could no longer jump on to the bed. She needed a box placed by the side to climb up.

It was at this nadir that Jack decided it was time to live in Europe, a dream he always had. Being from Ireland, Janet readily agreed. The timing was right. They made plans to live in Ireland. Of course, Gwennie would come, too.

Jack believed in the words of the French writer, Antoine de Saint-Exupéry, author of *The Little Prince*: "'People have forgotten this truth,' the Fox said to the Little Prince. 'But you mustn't forget it. You become responsible forever for what you've tamed. You're responsible for your rose.'" And Gwennie would come to learn that she was Jack's rose.

Taking a cat or dog directly from the US to Ireland was not so simple. One had to go through one company based in San Francisco, would cost about USD2200, and that cat or dog would have to go in the plane's hold. The airline could only be either Air Lingus or Turkish Airlines (?). However, if one took that same cat or dog to another country in Europe and then took that same cat or dog from that country to Ireland, it would cost nothing, and the poor thing could go under the passenger seat in front on any airline.

Jack remembered how much he enjoyed a trip to Portugal twelve years before. For USD2200, he figured they could have a nice two-week holiday in a wonderful country forgotten by the world. It was the beginning of August. While the owner was on his summer vacation; they stayed in a one-bedroom apartment above and behind the Museum of Ancient Art in Lisboa, overlooking the April 25th Bridge spanning the Tejo River, modeled on the Golden Gate Bridge in San Francisco. In fact, the same US construction company built them both. As for Jack, he felt as if he had come home. So much so, that he canceled his flight to Ireland.

After another hotel room, a very noisy apartment in Parede, and a dark, noisy house in the center of Cascais, they finally settled into the regal, calm, and quiet Estoril. Their new home was originally the magnificent palace of King Carol II, the second to last king of Romania, who lived there in exile from 1940 until he died in 1953. With her fluffy tail held high like a triumphant banner, Gwennie loved roaming the antique laden halls and the extensive garden at night, always with Jack close behind her.

After Jack realized he was once again in a bad relationship that was long overdue to end, he persuaded Janet to continue to Ireland, per her original plan. Jack became Gwennie's constant and sole companion. They were now close friends. The irony is by this time Gwennie traveled even more than her Iberian Lynx father Nuno and, even stranger, she arrived back to the exact same homeland of her beloved dad. But rather than living in the poor land of Xisto, needing to catch rare rabbits for dinner, she lived in a palace where her every whim was taken care of.

CHAPTER SIX

Gwennie has a Chinese passport with her photo in it, as a security precaution against another cat stealing her passport and trying to enter the country illegally. In her photo, she has a very grumpy face, having been rudely awakened from her important afternoon nap to have her photo taken. She also has two digital passports: one for the US and one for the European Union. And like modern spy thrillers, they are microchips imbedded between her shoulders.

The old Romanian King's palace in Estoril had fallen into near ruin after he died in 1953, like so many other grand manors across the country. By the time Gwennie moved in sixty-five years later, it had been completely renovated into twenty-five condominiums. Only six people, including Gwennie, lived there full time. The rest would come for a few weeks a year in the summer or for an occasional weekend.

The hallways and public spaces like the large dining room, living room with fireplace, game room, and other salons were all furnished in the original antique furniture with old prints of courtly life from many centuries before hanging on the hand-painted walls. Beautiful, well-kept gardens surrounded the palace. Gwennie would occasionally tell Jack that she was tired of being inside all day. Jack would escort her through the deserted hallways to the gardens. He would sit with her as she sniffed the flowers and wandered through the grass by the bushes. After an hour or so, she would walk back to their apartment with Jack following.

Otherwise, Gwennie enjoyed napping in the sun on her wide comfy chair in the corner of the living room. Jack would open all the double wide windows, making their home seem like it was practically outdoors. Just outside the windows beside Gwennie's day bed was a huge Night-Blooming Jasmine (Lady of the Night) flowering bush reaching the second floor above. It filled entirely their corner of the garden. Its branches full of small white flowers would pour in through the open window, filling the living room with its heavenly fragrance.

Often in the evenings, Jack and Gwennie would share a bottle of the excellent Portuguese wine and reminisce of their many past adventures. They remembered the different environments, smells, sounds, different cuisines, everything. Gwennie noted that in the US Jack would usually give her dishes of chicken or beef to eat, whereas in Germany it was turkey and rabbit, and in Portugal it was sardines and salmon.

The cans of wet cat food available represented the tastes of the local people and not necessarily the tastes of cats. The conclusion was the same for both: they had landed at the best place of all. Gwennie would often say that if the US cats had any choice, they would all be living in Portugal.

The almost always peaceful Estoril in the land of the calm and patient Portuguese was the perfect choice. Jack was no longer consulting on projects around the world. He was filling his days, finishing his first novel, and writing his second. Calm and peaceful was exactly what he needed. They were together every day, all day. Gwennie was the happiest she had ever been. She carried her furry dust sweeper tail high as she moved about her new world.

One day, after Jack returned from a walk along the ocean, he told Gwennie that he saw a man walking his dog. He was talking to his dog as if the dog could understand. We both had a good laugh over that.

After Gwennie regained her composure, she replied, "That's so absurd. It reminds me of the story of the talking dog. Have you heard this one? No? Well, stop me if you have.

"A man is driving through the countryside of the Appalachian Mountains in North Carolina on vacation. He sees a sign in front of an orchard farmhouse that says, 'Talking dog for sale'. He smirks at the idea, but curiosity gets the better of him. So, he stops and knocks on the door.

"An older man in overalls answers the door. The traveling man enquires about the talking dog. 'Yeah, sure, my talking dog. He's out back if you want to talk to him.'

"The curious man walks through the kitchen and out into the backyard. Sure enough, there is a large yellow dog napping in the sun on the grass near where the apple orchard started. He walks up to the dog, not sure what to do,

"Suddenly the dog looks up at him and says, 'Would you please not block the sun? Step to the side, if you don't mind.'

"The man exclaims, 'Oh, my God! You really can talk!'

"'Yes, of course I can talk. Is that surprising?'

"'Ah... Yes, it is extremely surprising. So, tell me about yourself.'

"'Sure. I started my career in the service of our country, working for the CIA. I traveled all over the world, listening to the meetings of our enemies. You know, no one ever thinks about the dog sleeping in the corner.'

"'After many years of that, I became tired of all the traveling. So, I worked as a Customs dog at the Port of Long Beach. You might have heard about me in the news about eight years ago. I found a shipment of cocaine with a street value of over $100 million. It broke all the records at the time.'

"'After some years of that, I decided I wanted to retire back home. I came back and found a she-dog. We had many young ones. She ran off with a younger dog. Women! I tell you! I prefer being alone anyway. Now I just rest here, thinking about the excitement of the old days. That's the short version. Anything else you want to know?'

"'No, but that's quite a story. I'll let you get back to the important work of sunning yourself. Have a good one.'

"He returns inside where the old farmer is sitting with a cup of coffee. 'That's incredible! Your dog really does talk. That's very special. So, why are you selling it?'

"The man answers in exasperation, 'Because he's a damn liar! He's never been off my orchard his entire life.'"

CHAPTER SEVEN

Often Jack would have dinner events in the Palace dining room for sixty or more people. Gwennie would come and join the crowd wandering through the many dozens of pairs of feet, eventually settling on the large yellow sofa in front of the fireplace with two adoring fans on either side, caressing her long magnificent fur. Once Gwennie's adoring attention meter was full, she would return to their apartment, finding the door left open for her.

Before going to sleep, Gwennie would share her observations of the various personalities and their quirks. There were those who drank too much and those who drank too little. A few talked mainly about themselves nonstop, and others were reserved, sharing little about themselves. There were those who knew how to pet a cat and those who did not, probably dog-people just being polite. Some were looking for men and others were looking for women. Some were looking for both. Jack listened quietly, rarely interrupting his observant friend.

"Jack, can you believe that a-hole Miguel? When it became his turn to introduce himself, he proudly told his stories of how he lived off of foreign women, until they would finally throw him out. I could not believe my pointy, furry ears! That's what he thought was most important about himself and wanted everyone in the room to know about him. He must be proud of his ability to attract the gullible and the foolish."

"Yeah, he was a strange one. I personally would have been ashamed to admit that. We are a business networking group and that's the service I guess he provides if anyone is interested in being used. After the presentation, he still had several foreign women of a certain age hanging around him. They seemed eager to be the next one to be used. I agree he is good-looking, but still."

"You remember that song where it goes 'I used her and she used me, but neither one cared'?

"I sure do, Bob Seger's 'Night Moves'. Here, let me play it for you." Jack concluded the subject as he reached for his guitar. As usual, Gwennie closed her eyes, contentedly listening to Jack's music performance for her.

When he finished, Gwennie continued her observations. "Did you notice that you also had your fair admirers? Seems like you could easily end your spell of being alone. For example, that sweet Portuguese woman who gave the presentation would be a wonderful possibility."

"Women admire men who are leaders. I guess they perceive me as being a leader."

"But you are, a natural one. You are the creator and organizer of popular events. Not many can pull that off several times every month."

"I just wanted something to do and meet people in our new home."

"Fine, but you're changing the subject. I just suggested a wonderful woman for you. My cat's sixth sense is telling me she's the one."

"Yes, I heard you. She does seem nice. I don't know. I guess I'm enjoying the peace of being unattached for a change."

"Fine, but I know you, Jack. You won't be alone for long."

In fact, there were many admiring women hoping for Jack's attention, Gwennie noticed. Jack noticed, too, but enjoyed being unattached for once, despite having many choices. The truth was Gwennie missed having a woman around. She never consciously thought about it, but she preferred the company of women. Perhaps it was their higher-pitched voices and their gentler touch. If she wanted to analyze it, she would admit it was because of Frank's brutal treatment of her during her first experience with people those many years ago.

Jack started a business networking group in both Lisboa and Cascais. Eventually, they would have 2500 members. He had the first Cascais event in the dining and living rooms of the palace. Over sixty people came. Each event had someone present their business idea and the others would give feedback and advice, even leads. Diana was the first to present her business idea for the Cascais group.

She was Portuguese and struggled a bit with English. But she was brave enough to present her idea of a longer stay business hotel that organized cultural and other events. Being very experienced in business, Jack offered to meet her sometime later to discuss her idea. She called a few weeks later and took him up on his offer.

They met at a seaside café in Guia high above the ocean just north of Cascais. After discussing her business idea for maybe fifteen minutes, their conversation drifted to music (they both considered U2 their favorite band), culture, their personal backgrounds, and eventually to plans to meet again.

It took a few more months before Jack realized that Diana was simply the nicest person he had ever met. After years of 'interesting' (meaning crazy) women, Jack finally had the wisdom of experience to choose kindness. Jack learned to tell himself, *"Let's start with being kind to each other and maybe love will follow."* Love did follow. Diana suddenly opened the doors to the Portugal of the Portuguese.

Gwennie loved Diana, too, though she never got there with Diana's three cats. Jack and Gwennie would spend weekends at Diana's home with a colorful, fragrant garden surrounding it. Gwennie tried to make friends with Malagueta, but she was too afraid of Gwennie, a cat twice her size. Caramel-colored Caramelo was curious about Gwennie like he was with everything. But he was a bit of a rough ruffian who did not understand how to communicate with the fairer sex. Gwennie would only hiss at him. Being male certainly did not help him. Cinnamon-colored Canela would only come home at night to eat, preferring to pass the days in unknown locations. Though she liked people, Canela loathed other cats. Gwennie never had a chance to be friends with her.

Nonetheless, life was so much calmer and quieter napping in the sun under the Night Blooming Jasmine on her little throne in the Romanian palace. Jack would be at his desk by the other window overlooking the garden. He was busy writing. After seven years, he finally finished his first novel, 'The Eye of the Beholder, International Suspense in the Art World (Illustrated)'.

During one of his seaside walks along the pedestrian only Paredão, Jack saw a poster of an Iberian Lynx on the stone wall with posters of other endangered animals. He could not help but notice the similarity between Gwennie and the lynx. Jack asked Gwennie about it and that is how he learned about Gwennie's Portuguese

Lynx father, Nuno, and her southern California Maine Coon mother, Terpsie.

He discovered all the details from Gwennie, who in turned had learned everything from long conversations with her father already eighteen years before. Jack thought the story was fascinating enough to write a novel about it. He titled it 'Nuno and Figo, The Strange Journey of Two Unlikely Friends (Illustrated)'. A professional Portuguese artist whom Jack met at one of his networking events illustrated it.

Jack continued with his third novel, 'Only After Dark, One Man's Descent into Obsession and Madness (Illustrated)'. He imagined his story of magical realism occurring in the very place and town he lived but forty-some years before, a few years after Portugal's Revolution. The palace was a ruin. Apparitions stalked the halls and the mind of the main character.

The idyllic days passed quietly. In the evenings, Jack would share with Gwennie the latest development in whatever novel he was writing. She would give him constructive suggestions about plot structure and character development. Jack would consider them but not always accept them. Even so, he respected her literary opinions. It was about a month after his third novel was published that life for both of them changed greatly.

CHAPTER EIGHT

After Diana's son moved out, her home was an empty nest. She decided it was time to fill her nest again with the man she loves. Jack agreed that it was time to live with the nicest, kindest woman he had ever met in any of the eighty-eight countries he had been. Gwennie and he moved into her house at the end of September.

It was challenging to shoehorn the best furniture Jack could offer, his other possessions, as well as Gwennie's things, into a house filled with nostalgic mementos from twenty-seven years of time. Diana had raised her two children there and had filled it with all manner of things no longer used but had strong sentimental value. In the end, they managed it well.

Gwennie had the upstairs as her primary domain, while Caramelo and Canela had the downstairs. Malagueta had since passed over the rainbow bridge to the next realm. So, the home had three cats again.

The main bedroom lost much of its empty floor space. Gwennie's large, covered cat box, tray of food and water bowls, her box steps leading up to the bed, and her soft bed by the door to the veranda laid a significant claim to the available space. Occasionally, Gwennie would wander to the other rooms, especially the dance room which had the large oriental carpet and white sectional sofa with the sheep skin she knew so well from her previous home.

The dance room was a room specifically used for dancing on Friday and Saturday nights. Diana and Jack would dance until the wee hours of the morning, barefoot on the white carpet. Gwennie would applaud sitting on the sheep skin on the sofa safely above the swirling feet. They used to dance in Jack's palace home like that. Gwennie was never one for keeping a rhythm, so she was content to just watch.

Age has a way of patiently stalking us. It degrades us physically slowly, barely perceptible, until one day we notice we simply cannot do the things we once took for granted. Gwennie's stalker was arthritis, hitting her hind legs particularly hard. She could no longer walk down stairs, except for the two by the bed. Even that was difficult for her.

Gwennie's mind was also losing its acuity. When they were still living at the Palace, Gwennie would go to her cat box to spring a leak, but would not get herself all the way in. She would leave a puddle of urine on the floor just below her box entrance.

This greatly irritated Jack. He showed her what she had done, putting her nose near her puddle like how puppies are house trained. Gwennie could only be embarrassed and apologize that she thought she was all the way in. Jack still had to get out the mop and clean up her mistakes.

Initially, Jack would follow Gwennie to her cat box and when he saw her backside hovering over the edge and her tail raised in preparation, he would gently push her further in. Sometimes she would fall on her face from the push, but this was a very imperfect and rude solution. This disturbed Jack, but he could not think of any other way. Even with this sad solution, Jack could not be there every time for her. Mopping the floor was lessened, but still not eliminated.

Finally, having the creative mind of a hominid, he thought of a creative solution. He found a plastic tray that he placed below her cat box entrance. This would collect her urine and Jack just had to simply transport it carefully to dump in his toilet and wash it off. He accepted the silver lining that he had less to scoop up when he cleaned her cat box.

Later, after they moved in with Diana, she took to laying in her cat box. She did not care that her large Maine Coon body was sharing the space with the little treasures she had left before. This strange new practice alarmed Jack.

He remonstrated with her how absurd that was. Jack would lift the cover of her cat box and gruffly tell her to get out. She knew it was time with much embarrassment to reluctantly abandon her little shelter and slink out. She could not tell him why she was doing something so crazy. In fact, her strange compulsion frightened her.

This went on for some time until Jack guessed what Gwennie really needed. She clearly yearned for a covered shelter. Jack took her soft blue cat cave out of the garage and replaced the soft folded blanket by the veranda with it. He took it away from her several years before because he did not like her being so antisocial and hiding away all day. But it was preferable to napping in her cat box. Gwennie realized that was what her strange compulsion was all about. She sheepishly thanked Jack for his insight into her slipping mind.

"So sorry, Jack. Please don't be angry with me. I don't know what is coming over me. I get confused easily. It hurts when I walk and I almost cry when I can no longer do the simple things I could do before. What is it, Jack? What's going on with me?" Gwennie started to cry.

"Oh, my precious Gwennie, don't cry. It's called old age. I, too, can't do many things I used to do in the past. I can no longer go jogging because of my ankle. I can't lift weights because of my shoulder. Until I found a specialist who prescribed me medicine, the arthritis in my toes and fingers prevented me from even walking or playing the guitar. Something as simple as chopping an onion was very painful. I could not even cook anymore."

That did not calm Gwennie. "But Jack! Just look at me! I can't reach anywhere but my face to wash. My once beautiful fur gets matted easily. I'm all a mess. Maybe one day you will kick me out like that bastard Ken did. I'm all old and ugly now. One day you will want a younger, more energetic, prettier cat. She might demand that you expel me." She broke off into sobs.

Jack held her, kissing her beautiful fuzzy face. "Now, now, my sweetest Gwennie. It's all right. I could never ever do such a cruel thing. I will give you the best old age: full of dignity, comfort, and love. I will carefully unmatte your fur with my fingers and give you treats for the bother. That reminds me. I believe you might agree it's time for a few treats." As always, treats made terrible things better.

Over time, Gwennie only moved from her cat cave to her cat box to her food tray just a dozen cat feet away from each other. One evening, Jack noticed Gwennie could not move her back legs at all. She would drag herself to these three destinations. It broke Jack's heart. He cried as he sat on the floor, trying to lift her back legs so she could walk normally. Diana and Jack took her to the emergency room at the nearby pet hospital.

There she spent the night under observation with a tube in one of her front paws. The next day, they picked her up. Gwennie understood that she indeed had a problem and needed to make some changes. Her doctor told Jack that he needed to give her special vitamins, and other non-prescription foods and treats specifically to help the joints of elderly arthritic cats. Gwennie was already eating special food to protect her kidneys.

These greatly improved her mobility, but only to the point where she could use her back legs again as before the crisis. She still had her arthritic problem. Jack decided that besides all the special supplements, Gwennie needed to exercise, not just her body, but also her mind. They began an exercise regime. Jack carried her downstairs and out the back door, setting her down in the garden. He made sure to close the back door so she would not be lazy and walk back inside the short way.

She had to walk around the house to the opened front door, through the dining room and kitchen to the stairs leading back to her sanctuary. She would take her time, rolling on her back in the sun, studying the many flowers that surrounded her, including insects and other curiosities. This was good to exercise her mind, stimulating her to consider other things than the darkness of her cat cave walls.

After she announced she had arrived at the foot of the stairs, she would wait for Jack to carry her back up and place her on the bed. Gwennie's exercise coincided with Jack making lunch for Diana and him. Diana was working from home. One day Jack was busy making lunch and was not paying attention to Gwennie needing to be carried back upstairs. After not hearing her reminding call, Jack wondered if she was still in the garden. She was not there, nor anywhere else on the ground floor. Jack was worried about her. She had fallen into the swimming pool once before. Had she done the same and drowned? She was nowhere.

Finally, it occurred to him to look for her upstairs. And there she was. Gwennie answered Jack's surprised stares, explaining that she was tired of waiting for him, and decided to climb the stairs herself. And so, Gwennie's daily exercise included walking around the house and up the stairs. It always saddened Jack to watch her struggle as she climbed each stair one at a time. It was all he could do to hold back a tear when he watched her walk unsteadily with a wobble in her hind legs, stopping every dozen steps to rest.

And then there was the issue of her claws. Jack trimmed them when they became too sharp, saving many sweaters from being ruined by claw-made holes when he picked her up. After they moved in with their beloved Diana, Gwennie stopped using the scratchy pad. This resulted in the old claws that would normally be removed by scratching being pushed out by the new claws replacing them from beneath.

Slowly the new claw would push the old one in a tight arc to where it would start pushing into her paw pads. Jack had to cut these old claws away. Gwennie always protested bitterly about it but had no answer to Jack's wondering why she never used her scratch pad anymore. Fortunately, all would be forgiven with treats afterwards.

One afternoon, Jack was cuddling her during an afternoon nap. Gwennie was washing Jack's beard with that special cat shampoo. Later, she combed it with her paws. Her rumbling purr massaged his heart. He was not getting much of a nap, but he did not mind.

"We've been living here with Diana for almost a year. How's life treating you?"

"Well, Jack, I just turned twenty-two the other day. Except for my arthritis and being slow-witted, I must say life is wonderful here. Life has been incredible ever since I ran into your house that rainy winter's night those eleven years ago. It was my cat's sixth sense working, and it has always served me well."

"I'm so glad you ran into my house, and I could give you shelter from the storms of a too-often precarious life. You have been a real friend. It's true. Life with me was not always calm and stable. But that's the life I've chosen. I apologize for that. Cats aren't meant to travel around the world often calling a hotel room their home."

"Oh, don't think that, Jack. I wouldn't have traded it for any other way. My dear old dad traveled to distant lands and always landed on his feet. He had no one to guide him except for a worldly ship rat. You were the best guide there could ever be. How many other cats can boast about the adventures that I've had? Besides, you're the best friend a cat could ever have."

"I will always care for you. Sometimes I even imagine with my over-active mind that if I was homeless sleeping in an old dirty sleeping bag under a bridge. We would share whatever little food we could find, and you would be with me in the sleeping bag, cuddling next to my chest, like we're doing now."

"Yes, my dear friend, and I would purr as happily as I am now." With that, she laid her head on Jack's arm and mixed her purring with a light kitty snore.

The End

FINAL THOUGHTS

Gwennie still lives in her idyllic retirement. She is surrounded by love and kindness, even more spoiled than ever. Many people are shocked by how old she is. Maine Coon cats can live into their thirties. One never knows. So, I say, she might outlive us all.

This is the second and final part of the story that started with the incredible journey of her Iberian Lynx father, Nuno. Please read The Adventures of Nuno and Figo: The Incredible Journey of Two Unlikely Friends (Illustrated).

https://www.amazon.com/dp/1735260622

Gwennie thanks you very much for reading her story and she trusts you enjoyed it. This is the result of many years of work. She asks you, dear reader, to please leave a thoughtful and considerate review on Amazon. These are especially important to the author. The link that will take you directly to the review page is below.

https://www.amazon.com/review/create-review?asin=B0BCS7NNBX

Also, please leave a review on www.goodreads.com.

https://www.goodreads.com/book/show/62340726-the-amazing-tale-of-gwennie

ABOUT THE AUTHOR

Born in Philadelphia, Thomas Murray is foremost a storyteller and has been writing all his life. He is the author of The Eye of the Beholder, The Adventures of Nuno and Figo, Only After Dark, and Ponce de León: A Modern Sequel. He currently lives in Portugal.

Having lived overseas for over twenty-five years on five continents and traveled to eighty-eight countries, he has trained his mind to be sensitive to the wide range of nuances and world views that make up the personalities of everyone he meets. Greatly appreciating global cultures, he includes many details about the places and characters to make readers feel they are part of the story.

He is currently considering which idea floating in the ocean of his mind he should bring to life in his next novel. When he is not writing, he is travelling and learning foreign languages, currently Portuguese.

You can learn more about the author and his writing at www.thomasmurraywriter.com

Please like his Facebook page: www.facebook.com/thmurraywriter

You can contact the writer at Bastet Publishing: info@bastet.ink

Also By the Same Author

The Eye of the Beholder, Bastet Publishing, 2020 (first in the Gwendolyn series)

A young art forger on the run …

Gwendolyn, a likable rogue with attitude, is secretly a successful fine-art forger rubbing shoulders with society's elite and shady art dealers. When she switches her painting with the original in a private home and escapes, she is confident with another successful heist. Until the next day when the owners are found murdered.

Framed for murder, she must travel to dangerous exotic lands to find the real murderers and clear her name. But as she delves deeper into the dangerous underworld of art forgery and betrayal, she realizes that she may be in over her head.

As the stakes get higher and her enemies close in, Gwendolyn must use all her cunning and skill to survive. Will she be able to untangle the web of lies and clear her name? Or will she become the next victim in a deadly game of cat and mouse?

https://www.amazon.es/dp/1735260606

Red Is a Color, Bastet Publishing, 2024 (second in the Gwendolyn series)

Is it a crime to be a redhead?

Gwendolyn, our favorite art forger and seductress extraordinaire, returns for another hair-raising adventure. Set in the sensuous backdrop of Portugal, Gwendolyn's latest project starts off as just another painting to forge and another wealthy eccentric to con. But as she delves deeper into the lifestyle of her unsuspecting mark, she begins to uncover more questions than answers.

How did he acquire a previously unknown Renaissance masterpiece by Botticelli? Why does he spend every evening worshipfully gazing at his personal goddess of love? Who is his tempestuous friend with an evil obsession with redheads? Who are the fanatical cultists trailing her every move?

The shadows of reality and myth blur, threatening to swallow her up in a deadly abyss… Will she survive this latest escapade with her life, much less her sanity intact?

www.amazon.com/dp/B0D64LM15C

The Adventures of Nuno and Figo: An Illustrated Journey of Two Unlikely Friends, Bastet Publishing, 2020 (first in the Gwennie series)

One clever rat, one tramp steamship, one hungry lynx …

Experience an adventure unlike any other. Follow Nuno, a clever Iberian Lynx, as he embarks on a treacherous journey to Southern California in search of a new life. Along the way, he meets Figo, a streetwise ship rat, who introduces him to the different cultures, music, and cuisines of the ports they visit.

Together, they face perils lurking around every corner as they form an unlikely friendship. Will it endure the journey, or will the dangers of California prove too difficult to survive? With beautiful illustrations by Madalena Bastos, this is a book you won't want to miss. The author will donate 10% of net proceeds to one or several organizations whose mission is to save the wonderful Iberian Lynx.

https://www.amazon.es/dp/1735260622

Only After Dark: One Man's Descent into Obsession and Madness, Bastet Publishing, 2021

Prepare to be enthralled by a dark and beguiling world as an American author of horror discovers an alluring and mysterious existence beyond his own in the post-Revolution Portugal of the late 1970s. Running from his past, he moves into an abandoned crumbling palace, eager to make progress on his next bestselling novel. A chance encounter with an unnamed, yet shockingly sensual woman pulls aside the veil of the world to reveal an alluring existence defined by unnatural delights and mind-twisting hedonism.

As his mysterious lover draws him further into her realm of shadows and ultimate pleasure, how much is he willing to sacrifice to keep her? And will there be anything left of his sanity when his would-be goddess is through with him? A tale told in the vein of Lovecraft and Edgar Allen Poe, this book will have you on the edge of your seat and wanting more.

https://www.amazon.es/dp/1735260673

Ponce de León: A Modern Sequel, Bastet Publishing, 2022

What is the meaning of life if you can live forever?

What if 500 years ago Ponce de León did discover the Fountain of Youth? He and his crew have everything anyone could dream of: wealth, health, love of friends, and time; eternal time. But is immortality a blessing or a curse? Ponce de Léon is not so sure. He enters a personal crisis seeking this answer to the meaning of life. His search for answers leads him to a truth he never expected.

https://www.amazon.es/dp/173526069X